I'm So NOT Wearing a Dress!

BY
Julie Merberg

ILLUSTRATED BY
Mai Kemble

downtown bookworks

downtown bookworks

Written by Julie Merberg
Illustrated by Mai Kemble

Designed by Georgia Rucker Design
Typeset in Museo

Printed in China
June 2010

ISBN 978-1-935703-05-1

10 9 8 7 6 5 4 3 2 1

Downtown Bookworks Inc.
285 West Broadway, New York, New York 10013

www.downtownbookworks.com

FOR SHELBY, MY SUPERSTAR NIECE
WHO NEVER WEARS A DRESS.

—J.M.

TO MY TWIN SISTER, MEI, MY FELLOW TOMBOY.
AND TO MY FAMILY AND FRIENDS
FOR ALL OF THEIR SUPPORT.

—M.K.

These are my
favorite shoes.
They are **PERFECTLY**
worn in and cozy.

They have **SUPER**
gripping powers that
help me climb trees.
And rocks.
And walls!

Plus, they are **TURBO-CHARGED** speedy! I can run so
fast in my sneakers that I am *never* "it" in tag. I can *always*
keep up with my brother, Alex (he's three and a half years
older than me). I am sooo much faster than the ball in
running bases! And I am usually the first one on my soccer
team to get to the ball.

My next door neighbor Sophie thinks my shoes are stinky, but I don't care.

She wears sparkly, pink shoes and a crown like she's a princess. She says it's a tiara and she wants me to wear one too.

I will wear a baseball cap. And I might wear a ponytail. But I will **NOT** wear a **TI-AHHHH-RA**. Sophie can play with someone else.

My friend Nate wears a baseball cap just like mine.
We dig for worms together. We keep the worms in a
bucket and build worm houses for them—it's easy!
All you need is mud, plus grass for the worms to eat,
and leaves for their beds. They get tired slithering
around all day.

My mom looks at my fingernails after worm-hunting. "Want to get a manicure, Shelby? Just you and me! And how about a pedicure while we're at it?" She asks me like I'm supposed to be excited, but I am not.

She promises to get me a donut, so I go with her.

My mom picks out cherry red polish for her nails. I pick blue and white stripes to match my favorite baseball team.

While Mom and I are drying our toes, Sophie comes into the nail place with her mom. I try to hide.

"Look, Shelby! I'm getting bubble gum pink!" Sophie tells me.

I can tell she doesn't really like my stripes.

CHECK OUT MY SUPERSONIC FAST BALL!

Nate and I can throw and catch 97 million infinity times without dropping the ball. Seriously.

Well, almost.

When Nate's next supersonic fastball
goes so far it lands on another planet
(seriously!), we decide to make delicious
mud pies. We mix the batter up with a stick.
    I offer Sophie a taste. I tell her it's yummy
and chocolatey!

    She doesn't realize I am joking.

Dad makes me apologize to Sophie. I even bring her a donut, but she doesn't believe that it really is chocolate this time.

When we get home, Mom cleans the mud
pie out of my fingernails and asks me to please,
please stop playing in the mud.

"Aunt Jen sent you a surprise," she
tells me. I miss Aunt Jen. I love surprises.
I wonder if it's chocolate.

Mom opens the box. "It's a cape,"
she says.

Hmm. A cape can be cool.
I like to play superheroes. I take
a closer look.

It's so not a superhero
cape. It's itchy. I will
definitely not be flying
in this itchy cape.

"It goes with this dress," Mom explains.

DRESS?!

She pulls a scratchy, matchy dress out of a box like it's a real present.

YUCK! I am NOT wearing a dress.

THAT'S A REAL BEAUTY!

I don't need any new clothes. I like wearing Alex's old stuff. His shirts are all soft and comfy and stripey. His pants are all cozy and holey and roomy!

LOOK, DON'T NEED GLOVES!

"Alex's things are too big. And they're all stained," Mom says.

"Those are fine for the playground," Dad says, "but every *now and then*, like for a *special occasion*, it might be nice for you to wear a dress."

Why do they suddenly care what I wear?
They're up to something...

I give them my scary look.
I *will* find out what's up...

"We're going to Aunt Jen's wedding next month. She really wants you to be a flower girl. All of your cousins will be there! Grandma will be there too. A photographer will be taking pictures," Mom announces.

"Being a flower girl is a really big deal. You walk down the aisle right ahead of the bride, spreading flower petals. Everyone will be watching," Dad adds.

So *that's* what's up.

Are they kidding me?

Mom is suddenly like a magician pulling shopping bags out of thin air!

EVERYONE WILL BE ALL DRESSED UP. THIS ONE WILL LOOK GREAT WITH YOUR HAIR.

YOU DO HAVE SUCH PRETTY HAIR!

IT'S SO FRILLY—AND SILLY!

IT'S LIKE A SWEATSHIRT!

THIS ONE FEELS REALLY SOFT.

IT'S PINK! IT STINKS!

I count to 10 and think about chocolate. Just like Mom tells me to do when I'm angry.

I have a much better idea.

I *really* hate dresses.
But I really do love
Aunt Jen...

We make a deal.